COLORADO MOUNTAIN BRIDE

MAIL ORDER BRIDES OF COLORADO

SUSANNAH CALLOWAY

Tica House Publishing
Sweet Romance that Delights and Enchants!

Copyright © 2025 by Tica House Publishing LLC

All rights reserved.

No part of this book may be reproduced in any form or by any electronic or mechanical means, including information storage and retrieval systems, without written permission from the author, except for the use of brief quotations in a book review.

PERSONAL WORD FROM THE AUTHOR

Dearest Readers,

Thank you so much for choosing one of my books. I am proud to be a part of the team of writers at Tica House Publishing who work joyfully to bring you stories of hope, faith, courage, and love. Your kind words and loving readership are deeply appreciated.

I would like to personally invite you to sign up for updates and to become part of our **Exclusive Reader Club**—it's completely Free to join! We'd love to welcome you!

Much love,

Susannah Calloway

SUSANNAH CALLOWAY

VISIT HERE to Join our Reader's Club and to Receive Tica House Updates!

https://wesrom.subscribemenow.com/

CONTENTS

Personal Word From The Author	1
Chapter 1	4
Chapter 2	15
Chapter 3	31
Chapter 4	39
Chapter 5	47
Chapter 6	56
Chapter 7	63
Chapter 8	71
Chapter 9	84
Chapter 10	94
Continue Reading…	97
Thanks For Reading!	100
More Mail Order Bride Romances for You!	101
About the Author	103

CHAPTER 1

The young woman took a deep breath to steady herself – and lifted her gaze.

She was met with the features she expected - rather ghostly pale after a long, hard winter. The dark brows arched over the wide brown eyes, drawn together at the ends to furrow a little over the bridge of the nose. Mouth wide and generously cut, though rather worn around the edges. Overall, the face of someone who expected the worst – based on experience.

Hardly the face of a woman who was mere moments from meeting the man she was going to marry.

With an effort, she smiled a little, but the resulting change in the reflection brought her no relief, and she abandoned the effort almost immediately. Better she should look worried, as she truly was, then try to hide her feelings. She'd never been very good at it anyway, no matter what Mrs. Pope at the finishing school tried to teach her.

It was no use putting off the inevitable any longer. With another deep breath, more quickly this time, she pushed open the door of the compartment and joined the small crowd that was making its way from the train.

Why anyone would choose to alight here, in such a dismal place, she could not imagine. The winter was still in full swing in Colorado. Her footsteps crunched on snow – snow that had once been clean and white and pure, but which was now decimated and stained by mud - footsteps of a dozen other passengers and more. The wind whipped at her, trying its best to steal her away – and if it could not steal Emma herself, it would settle for her shawl. She dropped her valise hastily to grab at it before it was carried away. She had few possessions and could not afford to lose anything that might keep her a bit warmer in the face of the, evidently, ongoing winter weather.

"Nobody," she murmured to herself between lips that were rapidly going numb, "would believe that this is the second of March."

But life here in Colorado was evidently quite different from the life she had left behind in Boston. Oh, there were cold winds in Boston, but there were buildings in which to escape them, a newfangled notion which had apparently not caught on here in Clem's Peak, Colorado. She was surrounded by – well, nothing at all, really. The wooden platform that constituted the train station had no ticket counter, no benches, nothing behind which to hide for protection. She squinted into the wind, her eyes streaming with tears; in the distance a little way, she could make out the shape of a few lone buildings.

That, she told herself, must be the heart of Clem's Peak.

The others who had disembarked, for whatever unfathomable reasons, had already dissipated, either taking themselves off to their own well-known destinations or met by welcoming friends and family. By now, there was no one there on the station aside from herself and a long-suffering porter, who handed her down her small suitcase and gave her a sympathetic smile.

"Know where you're headed, miss?"

She tried to stop her teeth from jittering.

"N-not exactly."

"I reckon you've got someone waitin' for you, don't you?"

She had no interest in telling everyone her business, but neither did she have any interest in freezing to death here on the platform, and the train was already making puffing noises that suggested it was building up steam to move along without her.

"I h-had expected to be m-met here."

The porter swam a watering eye over the empty platform, reaching the same conclusion that Emma had herself. He pointed in the direction of the buildings she had already spotted.

"McHale's General Store," he told her. "I reckon they can help you out. I'm a bit of a stranger here myself, or I'd offer. Go on, ask for Mr. McHale. He won't steer you wrong; he knows just about everyone who's born here in the county for the past fifty years. And," he added with another smile, "he'll give you a fire to warm by before you carry on."

Emma nodded.

"Thank you," she shouted above the wind. She averted her eyes to avoid yet another look of sympathy from the porter as she collected her things; after all, she knew how pathetic she must look, arriving in such a small, isolated place with no one to meet her. From the look of things, he must believe that no one cared about her at all. How surprised he would be, if he knew the truth.

Gritting her teeth, she clasped her valise in one hand, the small suitcase in the other. Between the two, they represented every possession she had left to her in the world, after the creditors had finished with her. Not that she had ever had much to begin with; the Potter family of Boston had never been noteworthy for their fortune. But things had certainly taken a turn for the worse after the death of her father – more appropriately, the long illness of her father, for which seemingly staggering sums of money had been promised to treat the symptoms if not the cause. And now here she was, hundreds of miles away from the home in which she had been born and raised. Her father was gone, his legacy was gone, her mother was a broken woman who had fled to the sanctuary of her childhood home to be looked after by her younger sister. Emma Potter herself was in Clem's Peak, Colorado, wiping tears from her eyes and forcing her way through the wind toward the mercantile, to beg strangers for an answer to why she had not been collected at the train station.

She had wondered why all the rest of her fellow passengers had disembarked here, in the middle of nowhere. She had thought that she had more of a reason to do so than they, but perhaps they had known something she did not. Perhaps she would find out.

The thought of her own ignorance, inexplicably, cheered her. Surely there was a reason why she had not been met as expected. It only remained to find out. With this fueling her limbs, she made her way a bit more swiftly through the muddy remnants of snow and the driving wind to the haven of the mercantile. McHale, whoever he was, had evidently not considered the denotation of his store to be of primary importance; or, which she considered more likely, trade in Clem's Peak was so miniscule and stagnant that everyone within a hundred-mile radius knew precisely where the only store in the county was located. Either way, it was almost impossible to make out the painted letters on the sign, but she managed and thrust herself in a frozen heap through the door into the blessed warmth within.

The man behind the counter – she assumed him to be Mr. McHale – looked up from his ledgers with a jovial smile.

"Come in, m'dear. What on earth is a little thing like you doing out there in the wind, I'd like to know. Come off the train, have you?" He had a rich chuckle, which he employed liberally as he half-carried her over to the stove in the corner. "I hope you weren't expectin' too much here in Clem's Peak, miss, for we haven't even a boarding house since Mrs. Benson closed last autumn. I can give you a stiff whiskey and last year's latest styles in hats, but that's about it. Or have you come expectin' to make your fortune in the gold mines?" He chuckled, taking a seat next to the one he had ushered her into. "I reckoned it was only a matter of time before the womenfolk got it into their heads to follow the example of the fellows and seek their weight in gold here in these brittle, brutal ol' mountains."

Finally feeling thawed enough to get a word in edgewise, she shook her head. "No, I'm not here for that, I'm afraid. Mr. McHale – you are McHale, aren't you?" A gentle nod was her answer; he didn't seem in the least bit surprised at her knowing his name without any introduction, but then, likely he was well-known in these parts and used to having his name tossed around. "I am hoping that you might be able to help me. You see, my name is Emma Potter, and I believe I am expected by Mr. Royal Monroe. Something must have occurred to prevent him from meeting me at the station, but..." She trailed off, staring wide-eyed at the store owner. The change in that genial, well-weathered face was remarkable – and startling. "Is something wrong?"

McHale shook his head slowly.

"I'm awful sorry to have to be the one to tell you this, miss," he said. "But Roy Monroe is dead – dead these past three weeks."

Emma felt her heart grow still and cold. Scarcely able to believe what she was hearing, she found herself unable to move, while McHale's words continued dimly.

"Most folks around here are half one thing and half another – Roy's no exception. He runs – pardon me, ran – his ranch enough to keep food on the table, but his heart was in these mountains...in the search for gold. Yes'm, Roy was a prospector, with dreams that dazzled, same's most men in the county. It was that hope that did 'im in, I guess."

"What do you mean, Mr. McHale?" Her own voice sounded faraway.

McHale rubbed his hands together slowly, clearly reluctant to tell her directly.

"The hills around here are littered with caves," he said at last. "That's where they found 'im. It was a slide took 'im down. I reckon he might have just disappeared if not for the fact that little Emily walked into town and asked for help when her pa didn't come back."

It was far from the first shock that Emma had encountered in this brief conversation, but it was the one that set her rocking back in her chair.

"Emily?"

"Think on it," McHale said hollowly. "Just seven years old and come to look for your pa and find 'im like that…nearly two days had passed by the time we figured out where he was. And poor little Tom."

"Tom?" Emma said stupidly. "He has – he had two children?"

"You didn't know? Oh, but maybe you two weren't all that well acquainted…" McHale rubbed his chin, eyeing Emma speculatively. It was now, she knew, that he finally began to wonder what on earth this young woman was doing here, disembarked from the train and asking after a dead man.

She steeled herself and clasped her hands in her lap.

"Mr. Monroe and I," she said, "are engaged to be married. Were, I suppose I should say. He paid a fee to a matrimonial agency in Boston, and I agreed to the match. I didn't know he had children. I didn't know he was a prospector. I certainly did not know that he was dead."

McHale leaned back in his chair, frowning thoughtfully.

"And now that you know, miss…I reckon you'll need someplace to stay tonight so's you can catch the train back east tomorrow."

It was a reasonable assumption, she thought. Nonetheless, it was wrong.

"Who might I hire to take me out to Mr. Monroe's ranch?" she asked firmly. The store owner raised his eyebrows, and she went on, though she knew she owed the man no explanation. "I was engaged to Mr. Monroe, and with or without my knowledge of their existence, I owe something to those two poor children. I have no reason to return east immediately; nothing is waiting for me there. There is clearly a need more pressing here in Colorado."

"I can take you," said another voice from behind her. Emma turned her head; she hadn't heard the front door open, but it was quickly clear why. This was a shop boy of sorts, and he had entered from the back of the store, carrying parcels in both hands. He lifted them in a gesture to McHale, then deposited them on the counter. "These came from the train, Bob. I'll deliver 'em tomorrow, if that's all right by you."

"Fine, Jerry, just fine."

The young man held out a hand to Emma, and she took it, expecting a shake; but instead he helped her from her seat. He had a very firm grip.

"Jeremiah Blake," he told her. "Happy to run you out to Monroe's ranch, whenever you're ready. I ought to warn you, though, miss. James Monroe isn't exactly the type to welcome guests."

She blinked at him blankly.

"James Monroe?"

"Roy's older brother. He showed up about a week ago to take charge of the ranch – and the children, I guess. He's their only living blood – that we know of." He scratched the back of his neck. "Their ma took off…what was it, Bob?"

"Right about five years ago," said McHale. "Can't have been more than six months after little Tom was born."

"And nobody's heard from her since," Jeremiah Blake said promptly. "I reckon those two little 'uns'll be glad to see someone in skirts for the first time in a long time." He gave her a grin. "Just don't say I didn't warn you about James."

Emma had a strong character, and she was not easily swayed from her purpose once decided. But at this moment, she had to confess to herself that she felt rather faint. Perhaps it was only to be expected – she had discovered that the man she was engaged to had two children and a brother, none of whom she had previously suspected, and in addition, he had been dead and gone for nearly a month. Why, he must have died around the same time that she first boarded the train in Boston. It all made her feel rather ill.

But there was nothing for it. She had set her hand to the plow, and she wouldn't look back now.

She gave Jeremiah Blake an appreciative nod.

"Thank you," she said. "I am ready now."

CHAPTER 2

"Another thing about James Monroe," Jeremiah said as the wagon ambled along the road west. "He's the quiet type. I don't reckon anyone's heard him speak more than ten words together since he arrived."

Emma knew that she ought to be counting her blessings; it was kind of the shop boy to volunteer to drive her to Monroe Ranch, and kind of Mr. McHale to allow him to without insisting that he first complete his duties. Overall, the folks she had met in Clem's Peak thus far were just that – kind. And Jeremiah's helpful hints about the situation she might encounter at the ranch were kind as well. But in the moment, she wouldn't have minded at all if he, too, were the quiet type, just so she had a moment of silence to wrap her mind around all that had happened.

Alas, such a gift was not to be given.

"I don't know much about him, myself," Jeremiah went on. "He lived over in Dugan, I guess, with his wife. That's about twenty miles from here. Something happened, they say, but I don't know exactly what. Anyhow, he was alone when he showed up here at Clem's Peak, and frankly from what little I've seen, I'm not too surprised." He glanced at Emma and gave her an ingratiating grin. "Not that there's a lot of pretty girls to go around, for all the bachelors in the county. You're a rare breed, miss."

His smile was undoubtedly flirtatious. Had she heard her confession to Mr. McHale about why she was here? If that was the case, then he knew she had been open to marriage and that her husband-to-be was no longer with them. If Jeremiah had been any less helpful or innately likeable, Emma would have taken offense at the ham-handedness with which he attempted to feel her out. As it was, she took a deep breath to forestall a snappy reply.

"Does he intend to stay and care for the children?"

"I'm not rightly sure. He ought to, I guess. But what that man thinks is anyone's guess."

She had no guesses of her own. For the children's sake, it would be best for their uncle to willingly take them in charge; then again, perhaps she shouldn't make such a judgement until she knew the man himself. After all, she had known plenty of unfit parents over the years. Fatherhood simply was not a given, in the modern world. She pushed the thought of her own father away and straightened up.

"How much further is it, do you think?"

"Not long now," Jeremiah said. "Matter of fact, here's the turn."

She was grateful for the prospect of bringing the journey to an end. It wasn't just that she was exhausted after the long train trip, though she was, but the frigidity of the breeze had turned her into a block of ice. Her shawl and the horsey-smelling lap rug Jeremiah had handed her simply were not doing enough. She clasped her hands in her lap beneath the heavy rug and made up her mind to endure.

The road wound around a clump of trees and a rocky outcrop. They were in hilly country. It was amazing, she reflected, how quickly the landscape could change from the flat emptiness of the town itself to these rocky, barren foothills, and the mountain range beyond. It was a wild and unknowable place, and the wind whistled through tree trunks and around boulders.

The cabin appeared quite suddenly. One moment it was not there, and the next it was. Jeremiah nodded toward it, but Emma already knew precisely what it was. Its very dilapidated state made it clear that it had not been cared for for some time. She had never seen a home which so clearly cried out for a woman's touch.

"The children live there?"

"Born and raised," Jeremiah agreed with a nod.

Emma clucked her tongue but kept her thoughts to herself. It would do no good to allow herself free reign, either of word or feeling. The most important thing was to ascertain that the children were healthy and cared for. After that she would consider the next steps after she had taken the first.

Jeremiah pulled the wagon to a stop, and Emma climbed down without waiting for him to offer a hand. Hands on her hips, she surveyed the scene. The cabin was made of rough-hewn wood planks, unpainted; the roof was shake, and several of the thinner planks had slid to the ground. It had evidently been a difficult winter. If not for the trees that were so closely arranged around the cabin, doubtless the wind would have taken more of the roof.

To her right, a small outbuilding stood. It was in no better shape than the house itself. A corral of sorts, made of split rail fencing, adjoined it.

"You said this is a ranch?" she ventured.

"Cattle," Jeremiah said. "Mostly free range. Looks like they've wandered off."

"I can't blame them," Emma said, despite her good intentions. "I would wander off, too."

If anyone was home, they would undoubtedly have heard the wagon pull up, have seen her step down and join them in the yard. But no one came out to greet them. Thoughtfully, she walked up the three steps to the door and knocked on it. Still, there was no reaction.

Jeremiah shook his head in return to her questioning glance.

"Do you suppose…" she said and broke off suddenly. A flash of movement caught her eye – something small and dark around the back side of the barn. She started toward it, and then paused, a finger to her lips thoughtfully. She turned back to Jeremiah.

"I don't suppose you have any idea where Mr. Monroe might be."

Jeremiah scratched his head.

"Like I said, the cattle are off wanderin', so he might be out after 'em. Or maybe…" He hesitated. "I hate to say it, but maybe he's as gold crazy as his brother was."

"I should hate to think so, too," Emma said softly. "Especially this soon after…" She paused again and tilted her head. "Do you hear that?"

She hadn't been aware of the steady sound until just that moment, when it suddenly paused. When it resumed, Jeremiah nodded.

"Reckon he might be around back," he said gratefully. "That's where the choppin' block is. Come on, miss."

He led the way; with another glance over her shoulder in the direction of the barn, Emma followed him. If the glimpse she had caught had, indeed, been the two children spying on the new arrival, she had no doubt that they would follow them to see what happened next.

Once they were around the back of the cabin and through a thin line of trees, she wondered how she had ever missed the sound of wood being chopped. It echoed from the steeply-rising hill before them; in the distance, she could make out a dark shape that seemed to lurk, which she realized only after concentration must be a cave carved out of the mountain – natural, perhaps, or the entrance to a mine. The thought gave her a tingle up and down her spine. She averted her eyes swiftly.

The chopping block stood next to a large pile of logs in various stages of decomposition – some of them had clearly fallen on their own and lain there for some time, others had been dragged. From the look of them, she would never have thought that they could be rendered down small enough for a woodstove – but if anyone was equal to the job, it was the massive, broad-shouldered man who stopped at the sight of them. He swung his axe over his shoulder and gave them a bold stare.

Jeremiah stepped forward.

"Monroe," he said with a nod. "I brought you a visitor."

James Monroe did not look like the type of man to appreciate visitors. He was almost startlingly large – well over six feet tall, sturdily built, and even the muscles in his visible forearms were impressive. He wore an old flannel shirt, sleeves rolled up to his elbows; a second flannel, of a different pattern, was visible beneath the tears here and there. His denim trousers were patched at the knees. For all his roughness, his unkempt appearance, Emma was surprised – and more than a little bothered – to realize that she found him attractive. Handsome, even, with his dark hair and black eyes and well-cut jaw. If only he weren't scowling at her as though her very presence offended him, she might have been even more complimentary.

"Not expecting anybody," he said.

Emma took a deep breath.

"Perhaps not," she said. "But your brother certainly expected me."

This clarification brought an even darker scowl, which she had not thought possible.

"What do you know about my brother?"

"Very little, evidently," Emma said. "But he *was* expecting me."

"Who are you?"

"My name is Emma Potter. I am – I was engaged to your brother Royal."

In one swift movement, James Monroe turned and brought the axe swinging down on the chopping block. Though the aged wood had clearly seen years of use and was something closer to a rock than a tree, the force of his blow sent the axe head cutting neatly through it like a hot knife through butter. The block split in two as cleanly as an egg.

"The *hell* you say."

It took all of Emma's self-control and courage to stand still and not to simply turn and run away. It would have taken even more to keep her from reacting in similar fashion – and she simply had no more to give.

"The hell *you* say," she retorted, hands on her hips. "Is that any way to speak in front of impressionable children?"

"What children?"

"Your niece and nephew – don't tell me you didn't notice that they've been watching us, hiding around the corner of the house. Or have you forgotten them entirely?"

James Monroe let the axe fall and took a step toward her.

"Now look here, lady…"

"Maybe we ought to come back another time," put in Jeremiah, trying to corral Emma and lead her back to the wagon. But she was having none of his efforts at pacification.

"As for your evident disbelief that Royal Monroe would be engaged, it's preposterous to even entertain such a notion. Why on earth would I, an intelligent, capable woman, come all this way on the pretense that I am engaged to someone I've never met?"

"Can't argue with that," said the elder Monroe brother, folding his arms.

"Good."

"Can't exactly swear that I know whether you're intelligent, for one thing. Or capable either."

"Why – how dare you!"

"Show me proof," Monroe demanded, his voice rising above hers.

Emma opened her mouth to retort that she had no need of proving anything – and then stopped abruptly. Reflexively, she glanced over her shoulder. Sure enough, two thin, peaky little faces looked out at her from around the corner, their eyes huge and dark with mingled interest and fright. Her heart tugged toward them, and she turned back to Monroe, lifting her chin.

"All right," she said. "Let's go inside and I will show you all the proof you could want."

He didn't seem over-eager to comply with her suggestion; but to his credit, he did so without any more fuss. The children scampered off ahead of them as they rounded the cabin to the kitchen door on the side. It was open, despite the coldness, and she was glad to see that he went at once to the fire to stir it up.

She turned to Jeremiah.

"Would you mind retrieving my valise?"

With a nod, he went off to fulfill her request. Feeling suddenly exhausted, she sank down into the chair at the table and took stock of her surroundings. The interior of the cabin, she was disheartened but far from surprised to see, was just as shabby and ill-kempt as the outside. Unwashed dishes were stacked on the table beside the wash basin. The floor badly needed to be swept. A pot of beans had boiled over on top of the range, leaving a dark brown stain that had not been cleaned up.

Worst of all was the state of the two children who now came forwards in response to their uncle's call, slinking out of the shadowy hallway to stand before Emma with their hands tightly clasped together. They both had the same dark hair as their uncle – obviously a family trait. But where Monroe's eyes were black as night, both children had gray eyes, wide and solemn.

Her heart in her mouth, she stared at them. With obvious uncertainty – but just as obvious intrigue – they stared back.

"Emily?" she asked the girl. Seven years old, McHale had said, but Emma would have guessed at least a year younger. She was very slight; though not so skinny, she was glad to see, as to suggest malnourishment. If the state of the children and the state of the dishes were anything to go by, at least James Monroe was keeping them fed.

The girl nodded.

"And Tom," Emma said, reaching out to touch the little boy's dirty sleeve. She smiled at them and was immensely pleased when he smiled back. The little girl seemed more worried, less inclined to respond in kind. "My name is Emma. I live in – used to live in Boston. Do you know where that is?"

Tom shook his head, but Emily said, cautiously, "It's a long way away – back east, isn't it?"

"It is, you're right. Two thousand miles away, in fact. Isn't that hard to imagine?" The children both nodded, seeming dumbfounded at the thought, and Emma risked a glance at their uncle. He was watching with a restraint that suggested he had decided to wait and see how things played out before he stepped in and separated them. As though he were watching a dog play with a cat, she thought with distaste. Why was he so mistrustful of her?

Jeremiah returned, carrying her valise. He set it down on the table in front of her and she opened it, reaching to the bottom for where she knew the letters waited. She pulled the packet out and held them for a moment, then looked up to Monroe.

It was an effort, but she managed to keep her voice steady.

"These are the letters your brother wrote to me. He applied to a matrimonial agency four months ago. I accepted the match, and we corresponded for a short time. I won't pretend that I had fallen in love with him – I don't know that anyone can grow to know someone else, over such a simple thing as a letter. And now that I'm here – why, I'm not certain that I knew him at all."

She held the letters out to him. For a split second, as he took them from her, she doubted the decision; suppose he was the sort of man to simply throw them in the fire and deny that they had ever existed. But he belied her suspicion of him and took a seat across the table, spreading them out. Drawn by curiosity, the children stepped up near him; Emily, Emma noted, put a hand on his knee quite unconsciously. It suggested that, at the very least, they were not afraid of their uncle, though he had only arrived so recently. It soothed her concerns – a little.

It struck her then that these two children had likely never seen their father's hand; and apart from the letters, they would never see that distinctive writing again. Her heart went out to them anew.

James Monroe read through the first letter and the second without comment; without any other noise except a snort or two of disbelief. By the time he reached the third, he put it down hastily when he was halfway through and looked up at her, shaking his head.

"You believed this pile of lies?"

"I had no reason not to," Emma said quietly. "The matrimonial agency had made the match; as far as I knew, they had ascertained that he was telling the truth."

"Matrimonial agency," Monroe muttered in dire tones. "Oh, I believe you now that you were engaged to my brother – my foolish younger brother. My only question now is whether you were equally a fool. He writes of owning the largest ranch in Colorado – of its beauty – the house is new, he says, but he won it in a poker game from an ancient prospector who likely built it some thirty years ago. The only thing holdin' this place together is stubbornness and spit. Wealth, fame, respect, honor…every good thing he says he has only exists in dreams. He says nothing of his first wife runnin' off, nothing of the children…" He shoved the papers back at her. "Lies. All lies."

Emma tensed her shoulders, realizing from the expression on Emily's face that she understood some of what her uncle was saying, even if not all.

"Mr. Monroe…"

"That's not true," Emily said stoutly, with more

determination than Emma would have expected from the frail little girl. "Pa was not a liar."

Her uncle turned a frown on her.

"He was, too," he said. "I knew him longer than you did, mind."

"He was *not*!"

"Mr. Monroe," Emma said again, more loudly this time. James Monroe glanced at her, one eyebrow raised, and she shook her head at him. "What good would it do, arguing with a child?" she asked him quietly. "What good would it do to insist on anything?"

"She ought to know the truth."

"And what good would *that* do her?" Emma countered.

Once more to her surprise, Monroe seemed to acquiesce, though he did not go so far as to agree with her aloud. Instead, he sighed and turned to Emily.

"Go on back outside," he said. "You and your brother. I'll call you in when supper is ready."

Emily nodded, but instead of immediately running for the door, she turned to Emma. For a moment, the two held gazes, and Emma was pleased to see another hint of that unexpected strength in the little girl.

"Were you really going to be our new ma?" she asked quietly.

Emma nodded.

"Yes, I was."

Emily glanced swiftly at her younger brother, who was watching her silently.

"Pa's dead."

Emma could not help but flinch.

"I know, dear. I'm sorry."

Emily took a deep breath.

"Does that matter? I mean – can you be our new ma anyway? We haven't had a ma…well, just about ever, I guess," she went on. "Neither of us remember. But it just don't seem fair, does it, that this should have happened? Tommy is only five years old." She put an arm around her brother's thin shoulders and drew him toward her protectively. "It just don't seem fair that he should have neither pa nor ma."

Emma had believed her heart to be beyond breaking. She had spent years, ever since leaving home, doing her best to build it up into something like steel. Now she knew she was wrong.

"No," she said softly, "it's not fair."

With a gesture from their uncle, Emily and Tom ran for the door and back out into the frigid air. Left behind, Emma and Monroe simply stared at each other for a moment. Even

Jeremiah was silent, seeming to recognize that this was a conversation he had no part in.

"Well," said Emma. She took the letters and folded them back into their envelopes. "Where does that leave us?"

Monroe bent his head to rub a hand through his thick dark hair. He sat for a moment in that attitude, then looked up suddenly.

"If you think those letters entitle you to somethin', you're mistaken. Besides, there's nothing here for you. This ranch is just about flat broke. We're barely hangin' on as it is. And as for the gold mine – that was nothing but a dream. A dream that brought my fool of a brother to an early grave."

"Leaving two small children," Emma said. "I don't want anything from you, Mr. Monroe, and I certainly don't think that I'm entitled to a red cent. Nor would I accept one if offered. But there must be something I can do, Mr. Monroe – for you see, I know what it is like to lose a father. And a mother, too. And Emily is exactly right – it isn't fair."

CHAPTER 3

"But I haven't anywhere to go."

"What's that matter to me?" James Monroe shoved the pot on the stove off the range. The liquid inside slopped over, and Emma pressed her lips together to keep herself from taking him to task for his slovenly habits.

"There's no inn or boarding house in Clem's Peak," she said. "I suppose you wouldn't know that, being new to the area."

"I know it well enough."

"So, my words are true, you see. There's nowhere for me to go."

Monroe stopped and stared at her for a moment, then glanced at Jeremiah. The shop boy stared blandly back at him.

"And my words are true, too," Monroe said. "Maybe you didn't hear 'em the first time around. What does it matter to me? You pointed it out yourself – I've got two little ones to care for, not to mention a ranch that's falling around my ears. The last thing I need is a meddling woman on top of it all."

He turned back to the stove and Emma glanced swiftly at Jeremiah, who nodded. Monroe's back was still turned, and he did not see Jeremiah slip out of the kitchen door. He was too preoccupied with his silly anger, Emma thought with a rather contemptuous pity.

"I haven't offered to meddle a bit," she said. "And if I was inclined to do so, I wouldn't stoop to meddling with you."

"I reckon you'd be quick enough to stick your oar in if you took a mind to it."

"You don't know a thing about me, Mr. Monroe, and I – will you *please* stop slopping soup all over the range? It'll just burn, and you'll be left with a terrible smell." She pushed him aside from the stovetop and reached for a dish towel to wipe up the mess. The towel was dirty, but it would do what needed to be done, she decided. Clearly, keeping up on the laundry was far from a priority in the Monroe household.

He snatched the towel back.

"This is you not meddling, eh?"

"It's not meddling, it's simple common sense."

"And who asked for it?"

"Clearly, it's a foreign concept to you, Mr. Monroe."

"I reckon that's just about it," he said suddenly. Two large hands closed over her waist, and she found herself abruptly hoisted into the air. Despite the suddenness of the movement, his touch was surprisingly gentle, and the squeak that she gave was of shock rather than pain. Before she knew it, they were outside on the veranda, and he set her down on her feet with a thump.

"Now, you just get back in the wagon and head on back to town. Hop on the next train east."

She folded her arms, deciding that it was beneath her dignity to accost him for lifting her. Besides, there were more important things to discuss.

"What wagon?"

James Monroe stared, wide eyed, at the place where the mercantile delivery wagon had been – and where it was no more. Jeremiah had left without saying goodbye, after depositing Emma's trunk on the steps.

"Why, that little..."

"Little pitchers have big ears," Emma said. Indeed, the children had appeared as though by magic, out of nowhere. Emily watched her uncle as he struggled to control his angry cursing, and Tom stepped close to Emma. To her surprise, and great delight, the little boy slipped his hand in hers and turned a sunny smile up toward her.

"Goodness," she murmured, fighting the urge to wrap both arms around him and press him close. It would never do to become too attached, too quickly. After all, she had no intention of staying here at the ranch.

Not for long, anyway. Just – just long enough.

"Did Jeremiah go back to town?" Emily asked innocently.

"And left us a delivery we didn't ask for," Monroe said snidely, glaring at Emma.

She blinked back at him.

"I certainly didn't ask Jeremiah to do any such thing."

"He heard you sayin' maybe you ought to stay."

"It was simply an idea."

"Well, it's a bad'n."

"I think it's a good idea," Emily said softly, but her uncle paid her no mind.

"And now," he complained, "I've got to go and roust out the horses to hitch up and drive you back into town. If it was an inch less than five miles, I'd make you walk yourself."

"Don't trouble yourself," Emma said mildly. "I have a proposition to make."

If she had believed that James Monroe's displays of temper were significant before, it was nothing compared to the thunderous way his brow furrowed, a light leaping into his eyes.

"I ain't gonna marry you, Miss Potter." The words came so furiously from lips drawn so tight that they were difficult to make out.

"I should hope you would never think of such a thing," Emma said tartly. "I wouldn't marry you if you were the last man on earth. But you are the guardian for these two children, who have only recently lost their father. I suppose their mother is unlikely to be located, which means that you, Mr. Monroe, have sole charge of them. Correct me if I am wrong, but you do not seem to know the first thing about being a father. You're rough, and rude, and inclined both to anger and to swearing. The house is a mess and the state of the children a disgrace."

His anger was beginning to bubble over by this point, so she lifted a hand in the hopes that it would bring it to a simmer. "I would venture to guess, however, that you might be very capable at running a ranch, given the opportunity. But taking care of two children on your own, as well as a household sadly in need of assistance, does not lend itself to other occupations. Therefore, my proposition is this." She fixed him with her gaze, steely-eyed, matching the furious light in his black eyes with her own. "I will stay for a month. During that time, I will care for the children and put the house to rights. You, meanwhile, will be free to concentrate on the ranch. You said yourself it's falling down around your ears. I suppose your brother was not proficient at running it adequately. Well, now is your chance to resolve the issue – with the added benefit of an *intelligent, capable* woman to run the household."

She could not stop herself from stressing the qualifiers; at this point, her exhaustion had settled into the background, giving way to a renewed energy that she knew would shortly lead to collapse, if she did not get some rest. The last thing she wanted to do was face the drive back into town, especially with only the prospect of some kind stranger's sofa to lay her head on. "And," she went on as inspiration struck, "I won't even require the usual salary received by housekeepers. I'll settle for that of a governess – it's far more attainable for someone in your position."

For a long moment, James Monroe simply stared at her without speaking. There was still fury in his eyes – and perhaps, she thought worriedly, she had come on a bit too strong.

"Pa wanted us to have a ma," Emily said quietly. "He would have wanted us to have a lady in the house – even if only for a little while."

James Monroe turned his black eyes on his niece, and Emma hesitated, torn between stepping forward to get between them and waiting to see what might happen next. But the reaction of the angry man surprised her; rather than grow even more irate at the defenseless girl, his eyes, impossibly, softened.

"No wages," he said. "Can't afford it."

"Fine, then." Emma felt rather light-headed. She certainly hadn't truly expected to be compensated for her work; it would be enough that she had a roof over her head and food in her belly, and that she could take a little time to consider her next move. James Monroe opened his mouth, then closed it again and stared at her.

"You don't care about that, do you?"

Emma shook her head.

"Not in the least," she said.

Those black eyes narrowed, squinting at her as though to see straight through to her soul, and she held her breath, fighting against the strange urge that stirred within her – the urge to step forward and open her arms. To what purpose? She could not be sure. To see what he would do with such an invitation, perhaps.

The thought made her shiver a little.

Then he turned away, breaking the spell.

"All right," he said. "One month. No more."

He stomped back into the house. Left on the veranda with her luggage, Emma turned to the children and was heartened to be greeted with two tentative, shiny-eyed smiles.

There was no need to hold back with them, she decided. She flung her arms open wide.

It went straight to her heart to feel them both leap forward into her embrace.

CHAPTER 4

Emma Potter had never considered herself to be the maternal type. If there needed to be some sort of label on the sort of woman she was, she supposed, she could do no better than "big sister." Though, she reasoned, she could certainly do worse. Older sisters were the ones who by turns teased and lectured, hugged and disciplined, led by example and joined in frivolity. Her days at the finishing school, long ago, had been marked by similar relationships – the younger girls who were far from home, missing their mothers, or afraid of the over-strict headmistress inevitably found their way to Emma.

It was much the same with Emily and Tom. Though she could not describe her feelings toward them as motherly, there was certainly a sympathy for their plight, a desire to make things better – and a rather fierce urge to protect them from further harm, whether that comes as the result of the big bad world as a whole or specifically at the apparently careless hands of their uncle.

And careless he indeed was, as far as she could tell.

He was a slob, for one thing – if anyone had ever expected the two children to pick up after themselves, it certainly would not be because of the model James Monroe set for them. Only two days into the month allotment, and she felt she was cleaning up after the grown man just as often as after the children.

Though annoyance stung at her, she did her best to bite her tongue and keep the peace. For the sake of Tom and Emily, if nothing else – certainly not out of consideration for Monroe.

As far as keeping house, she knew herself to be quick, orderly, and rather no-nonsense. It wasn't difficult to be quick; the cabin was rather sparsely furnished, and dusting hardly took any time at all. Besides the sitting room and a small study which did not appear to have been used in some time, there were three small bedrooms upstairs – one of which the children now shared, in order to make room for their new nanny. By far the most comfortable, cheeriest room in the house was the kitchen, which took up half the first floor. She spent most of her time there, and the children along with her, learning how to bake and cook and stir and clean.

But simply dusting and setting things in order was clearly not enough if she was to bring the house to standard. On the third day, she set herself to a serious deep clean of the rest of the house. She decided to start with the abandoned study.

It was obvious from the moment she set foot inside the little room that no one had used it since the former owner of the house had passed away so unexpectedly. There were papers spread over the little desk, a few books leaning haphazardly propped up against a makeshift shelf. Everything was covered in a fine layer of dust. She took a deep breath, struck by a chill. It must have looked precisely like this, the last time that Roy Monroe had been here. Perhaps he had been in the middle of some task or other and called away by the children. Perhaps he had planned to go back and finish it, tidy things away – and now he never would.

She rather doubted that he'd had any such intentions. The house would not have reached this state of unkemptness in only three weeks. The untidiness must stretch back much further than that – likely, she thought, back to when Roy's wife had left him. What had happened? The children were too young to know, and she certainly did not feel inclined to ask Roy's older brother.

With a sigh, she began to sort through the papers on the desk. Many of them seemed like little more than trash – advertisements, out of date newspapers, clippings of a serial. Underneath a five-month-old copy of *The Farm Journal*, she stopped suddenly as her sifting revealed a photograph. It was too small to make out the features as clearly as she would have liked; wiping the dust off with her fingertips, she took it over to the window to look at it in the light, which helped a little. Of the faces of the four people thus revealed, only one was at all familiar, though she couldn't place it at first.

Then the penny dropped. It was James Monroe, of course. She simply did not realize it because the man in the photograph was smiling.

Younger, too, she noted. She could guess Monroe to be somewhere around thirty, but this must have been taken a good ten years before. And the man beside him, with strongly marked features that were quite similar and yet undeniably different, was even younger, perhaps eighteen.

Royal Monroe.

For the first time – and the last – she was looking on the face of the man she had agreed to marry – the man that, in another world, would even now be her husband. She studied his features, probing her own feelings at the same time. She expected to feel some stirring of emotion, an incipient longing, a creeping regret. And yet she felt nothing apart from an impersonal interest. She had agreed to marry him. She had written him letters – and the letters he had sent her in reply had been decried by his own brother as a pack of lies.

She shook her head stubbornly, though there was no one to see the gesture. James Monroe's claims were far from verified, she reminded herself. She was inclined to disbelieve them simply out of dislike for the man, but quite apart from that, Roy Monroe could no longer speak for himself. The question of why, precisely, James Monroe would label his dead younger brother so vilely was far from settled, but she decided to ignore that. There was no telling what that man would do, or why, as far as she was concerned.

She looked over the features of Roy Monroe once more, recognizing now how much of his appearance had been passed down to Emily and Tom. And the young woman beside him – their mother? She was slight and rather plain, and there was a possessiveness to the way her hand curled under Roy's arm that made Emma quite certain that she was once Mrs. Monroe. As for what had happened to her – well, no one seemed able to answer that question. She would have to ask elsewhere, if she truly wanted to know; and she wasn't certain that she did. The issue of whether Royal Monroe had been eligible to marry without committing the sin of bigamy belonged to the matrimonial agency to settle.

Her eyes drifted back to the other couple. James, too, stood close to a young woman; she was rather pretty, with dark hair and wide dark eyes. She didn't stand in the possessive attitude of her sister-in-law, but her head was turned slightly, and her gaze fixed on the man beside her. There was no doubting the look of love in her eyes.

And what had happened to Mrs. James Monroe?

Why were the women of this family such a mystery – unless their disappearance could be blamed on the uncouth nature of their husbands?

She shook her head and set the photograph carefully to the side. As she combed through the next set of papers and detritus, she was disturbed to realize that her gaze returned again and again to the smiling, dark-eyed older Monroe.

Nearing the bottom of the pile, she spied a stack of letters tied up with piece of twine. Her first thought was that they were her own letters written to Royal; with a feeling of pleased recognition, she took them up and sat down on the rickety chair to look through them. But at once she knew that she was mistaken. The handwriting on the envelopes was certainly not her own; and the letters had been posted from other towns in Colorado, the names of which she did not know.

As she looked through them, her heart began to beat faster.

R. Monroe,

The terms of your loan are up. We expect payment by the beginning of next month. Remit in care of D. Jones, Denver, CO.

Angliston and Co.

Mr. Monroe,

I reckon you know that you're a month past due. We've done business together before, and out of respect for our history I'll let the month slide. But a good businessman can't look the other way forever. I didn't get where I got by letting folks take advantage. I want the money you owe by next week, even if you have to ride it here yourself.

Signed,

J. Packard

Monroe –

If I don't get the money you owe me by the end of the month, I'll come and collect it myself. I don't want any more guff about how that mining claim of yours went bust. I gave you that loan in good faith. If you don't pay it back, I'll take it back in bad.

-Billy

Letter after letter, the threats increased. Trying to control the jolt of fear in her throat, Emma spread the letters out on the desk in front of her. Some were repeated calls for repayment from the same loaner – others were simple threats to have the law called in on behalf of the injured party. All in all, it appeared that Royal Monroe had owed money to some six different parties.

Some of the funds, she realized, must have gone toward the fee required by the matrimonial agency. She was here because of these unpaid loans – and the thought made her feel rather ill.

She stood up hastily, feeling the urge to go to James Monroe with the letters and ask him what to do. At the very least, she owed him an apology – evidently, he had been telling the truth about his brother being a liar. And what of this mining claim that was mentioned in several of the letters? Perhaps Roy had been promising repayment based on the fortune he expected to find – but the mine had produced nothing. What then could he offer them?

After a moment of hesitation, she shook her head and gathered the letters together, shoving them into a single large envelope. No, she would hide them away, without telling Monroe. There was no reason to involve him, after all. Telling him he had been right all along would only make him more disrespectful of the dead – not to mention feed his ego.

Besides, it was all in the past. Royal Monroe was dead. What could his creditors do to him now?

CHAPTER 5

On the sixth day after Emma took up her temporary residence at Monroe Ranch, she knocked on the door of the bedroom belonging to James Monroe. It had taken several moments to work up her courage to do so – and now, with no response, she was far too keyed up to simply let it stand. Taking a deep breath, she flung the door open wide and barged in.

"Rise and shine, Mr. Monroe."

"Wha-"

Without letting him have a chance to react, she hastened across the room and flung back the curtains, letting in the weak sunshine of early spring.

"Good morning," she caroled, rather desperately. "Do you know what day it is?"

She turned around to face him – and stopped in her tracks. James Monroe sat up in bed, back against the headboard, staring at her balefully. He was bare-chested, his dark hair tousled from sleep, and she had a feeling that if he could have done such a thing by mere force of will, she would have erupted into flames.

"Sunday," she said, since he did not appear inclined to speak. "The day of the Lord, Mr. Monroe."

"Bah," he said sourly.

"I expected you'd say as much," Emma told him sweetly. "But be your heresy as it may, the children and I require a ride into town so we may attend church. No, I won't force you to do so yourself…"

This earned a scoff from him – almost a chuckle.

"You could try," he said.

"I have no intention of doing any such thing," Emma said. "As far as I'm concerned, your soul is your own lookout. The children, though, need a religious education. You are their guardian, which makes you responsible to see to it. I suppose they haven't been to church since their father died."

Monroe curled his lip.

"I don't reckon Roy was all that regular a church-goer."

"Hmm. Well. Better late than never, they say." She tossed him a clean shirt and made her way back out of the room. "We must leave in thirty minutes. Breakfast is waiting."

Not until after she was safely downstairs did she allow herself to breathe again – and to register at last how swiftly her heart was beating.

Despite his obvious anger at her waking him up on a Sunday morning, James Monroe appeared downstairs in less time than she had expected. He ate quickly, bolted a cup of coffee, and left again without saying a word. Emily and Tom turned worried looks on Emma, and she smiled at them reassuringly.

"There, now, are you all ready? Wonderful. I believe your uncle just went to hitch up the wagon."

And, indeed, that was precisely what he had done. The five-mile drive back into town was rather silent, apart from the whispering between Tom and Emily about what they might expect at the service. It was painfully clear that they had not attended previously; Tom thought it would be like a bazaar, and Emily questioned whether they would allow children in at all.

Monroe pulled the horses up a ways down the street from the little church and nodded them toward it.

"Go on," he said.

"Won't you come, Uncle James?" Emily asked, but he shook his head at her.

"They don't want the likes of me in a place like that. I'm smart enough to know where I'm wanted." He caught Emma's eye, and a fiendish half-grin appeared on his lips; by this time, she knew him well enough to realize that it signified he was about to try and get under her skin. "You can find me at the saloon when you're ready."

She narrowed her eyes at him, but it was obvious that he was pushing for a reaction – and she was determined not to give it to him.

"Very well," she said. "Come along, Tom, Emily. You'll have to introduce me to everyone you know."

With the children's hands in her own, she marched them off toward the open doors of the church, not deigning to glance back over her shoulder.

They were late, and the service had already started. As she hustled the children into an empty spot at the back of the little church, she was painfully aware of the dozens of curious glances sent her way. But it was only to be expected. Everyone knew Tom and Emily, of course, and doubtless knew of their father's untimely demise. Their sudden appearance with a stranger would undoubtedly raise a few eyebrows.

The church was quite full, to her surprise; there must have been more locals than she would have guessed from the size of Clem's Peak itself. Trying to pay attention, she found herself counting and reached thirty-three before the service ended.

One of the thirty-three congregants, a rather overweight, middle-aged woman who was seated in the second row, hurried toward her as soon as the prayer was over.

"Excuse me. Yoo-hoo!"

Emily spotted her at once; judging by the small smile that appeared on the girl's thin face, Emma guessed that the woman was at least known to the children. She waited politely as the woman huffed up to them and beamed down at them.

"Emily. And little Thomas!"

"Good morning, Mrs. Henry," chorused the children.

"Goodness, it seems years since I've seen you – but I suppose it can't really have been that long, or you'd be taller than I am, eh, Thomas?" She reached out to ruffle the little boy's dark curls, and sighed. "I've been meaning to get out there and inquire after you myself, but time simply gets away from me. The duties of a mayor's wife are never done."

Having tossed out this invitation for comment, she turned expectantly to Emma.

"Are you the mayor's wife?" Emma asked, feeling like an obedient child herself. "I'm afraid I'm not from around here and have only been here a week. I'm still quite a stranger."

"I thought I would have remembered meeting someone like you, m'dear – we've scarcely any young women here in Clem's Peak, and of course you're very pretty. How very kind of you to bring the children with you to church. Are you a relative?"

Steeling herself, Emma explained her presence. As she told the story, as briefly as she could, the older woman's face went from eager curiosity to open-mouthed astonishment.

"And Roy had planned to marry a mail order bride. Why, I never would have guessed such a thing. He was a nice man, of course, but poor as a church mouse, and too clever for his own good, always intent on some scheme or other." It was clear that she was poised to say more, but she stopped abruptly and glanced at the children. Taking her meaning, Emma crouched down to speak to Emily and Tom.

"Would you two like to go and find your uncle James?"

"In the saloon?" Tom asked, eyes round as marbles.

Emma pondered whether the shock to James of the children showing up in the saloon would outweigh the responsibility of sending them there in the first place.

"No, not inside, please," she said. "But if you stand outside and yell his name, I expect he'll come out right away."

She stood again and watched as the two children scurried off, hand in hand, clearly delighted with the mischief of this errand.

"And how do you find their uncle?" asked Mrs. Henry, a curious gleam in her eye.

Emma considered the merits of absolute honesty.

"I find him rather difficult, I'm afraid," she said at last. "But he does seem to have his good qualities – it's only that they're hidden under some which are less favorable. I can't pretend that he has made a good impression on me, overall."

"I was afraid that would be the case," the mayor's wife said sympathetically. "I have heard that he can be rather… truculent was the word, I believe."

Emma hid a small smile.

"I can imagine the locals here using other descriptors."

"Well…yes." Mrs. Henry chuckled. "But then, hardly anyone knows the truth about the elder Monroe brother. He's only visited once or twice since Roy bought the ranch, and I should say that he's quite different now than he used to be. Of course, there was that tragedy with his poor wife…"

Emma raised her eyebrows.

"I'm afraid I don't know anything about it. If hardly anyone knows about James Monroe and his history, I should lay the blame squarely at his door, for a more close-mouthed man I've never met."

"Perhaps – but it was truly sad, m'dear, so perhaps we ought to give him a little leeway, don't you think? His wife of five years…" She sighed and shook her head. "I've heard tell that they were very much in love. They lived up in Dugan; he was a doctor there and traveled all over the county. Wild territory, far wilder than here. One night, he was called out to attend a childbirth, and while he was gone, Mrs. Monroe went to visit a sickly neighbor in turn, since he was not there. A kind woman, they say. But…there was an incident."

Emma sucked in a breath, staring at the older woman. With a sinking feeling, she knew what was coming next – and did not want to hear the words. But there was no stopping Mrs. Henry now.

"A notorious outlaw robbed the neighbor's ranch, and when Mrs. Monroe tried to protect her poor friend, she was shot and killed. An instant death, they say, and painless – but not so for James Monroe. They say he blamed himself, for Mrs. Monroe would not have gone to help the neighbor if he had been at home." Her voice lowered. "It wasn't until after her death that he discovered she had been expecting."

Emma covered her mouth with her hand.

"That's…"

"Terrible, I know." Mrs. Henry shook her head sympathetically. Suddenly seeming to realize that they were still in the middle of the church, she stood up straight and offered Emma an arm. "I'll walk you out, my dear. I didn't mean to upset you."

Emma blinked back the unexpected tears that stung the back of her eyes.

"I'm quite all right," she said, lying bravely. "It was an unexpected story, of course, and quite – terrible."

"But perhaps it might make you think a little differently of Mr. Monroe," suggested Mrs. Henry.

The man in question had emerged from the saloon. He stood across the street, near the wagon, waiting for Emma to appear – and entertaining his niece and nephew, evidently, for Emma was surprised to see Tom laughing outright and Emma twirling around her uncle. As James Monroe turned his head, she saw that he was smiling. Her heart felt a pang, and she arrested her quick step in his direction.

"Yes," she said. "It might."

CHAPTER 6

The drive back to the ranch was far livelier, as Emily and Tom expounded at length on what they had learned at church.

"We all have an angel," Emily said with the air of a lecturer, "and they have wings and feathers and harps. I wonder if mine will teach me to play the harp?"

"I'd rather he taught me how to fly," Tom said candidly. "Uncle James, Pa always told me that I shouldn't say *Jesus* like he did. But the preacher said it over and over. Musta been a dozen times. *Jesus!* Just like that! If the preacher says it, Uncle James, it can't be that bad if I say it."

Emma hastily covered her mouth with her hand to hide her smile; when she glanced sideways at James Monroe, she was unsurprised to see that he wasn't trying to hide his grin at all.

"I hope your hour at the saloon was as elucidating as ours," she said, in a weak attempt to change the subject.

"I reckon I heard a few folks mention Jesus, too," said Monroe piously.

As they approached the ranch, though, the mood changed abruptly. Monroe sat up straight, his dark eyes peering keenly ahead. The children, seeming to realize that something was wrong, quieted down.

"What is it?" Emma asked.

He shook his head.

"Someone's been here," he said.

"How…"

"Don't ask me how I know. I know."

Try though she might, she could see no disturbances in the grass or mud that would have been caused by any tracks but their own. But he pulled the horses up abruptly beside the barn and leapt out. As she helped the children down, he returned from the barn with a frown on his face.

"Maple Sugar is gone."

"Hmm?"

"The brown cow. Dairy cow. She's gone."

"Are you sure that…"

"Roy let most of the cattle roam," he cut her off shortly. "But when I got here, I pulled her back home, so the little 'uns would have milk every day. Someone let her out. Left the gate wide open."

"Emma! Uncle James!" Emily ran back toward them from the direction of the cabin. A paper fluttered in her hand, and she pressed it to her uncle. "There was a knife," she panted. "It was stuck with a knife to the door."

He read it over with a flicker of his dark eyes and swore.

"What is it?"

Emma snatched it from him and read it swiftly.

Monroe owes – we collect.

Frightened, she looked at James Monroe, swallowing past the lump in her throat.

"Is this…"

He shook his head, seeming frustrated. "I don't know what the hell they're talkin' about. I've been here two weeks now, haven't borrowed anything from anyone. Haven't even asked for help with the children. If someone's got it into their fool head that they can kick a man when he's down…"

She swallowed hard.

"I think I know what it is referring to."

His eyes fixed on her with a suddenness and intensity that made her feel like stepping back; but there was nowhere she could go to escape the weight of that heated gaze. Besides – she didn't want to.

She pressed her lips together.

"Come on," she said.

It was difficult to distract the children from following them; not until Monroe told them sternly to go and play or he'd give them chores to do instead did they scatter, casting curious glances over their shoulders. She led him into his younger brother's study and dug the letters out from the bottom drawer of the desk, passing them over with a square of her shoulders.

"I ought to have shown you these before. I'm sorry. I didn't know what to think – but I certainly didn't believe that I was putting anyone in danger."

Brow savagely furrowed, he tore envelopes and paper in his haste to read through them all. At last, he slammed them down on the desk and swore again. She flinched a little, and he looked up swiftly as though he had struck her without intending to.

"You're right, you ought to have told me," he said. "But I don't blame you for not. You and I – well, we haven't been on the best of terms, have we? Haven't exactly been fightin' on the same side."

She managed a small smile.

"Sometimes I'm not even certain we're fighting the same war at all," she murmured.

He nodded in acknowledgement.

"But I reckon we can both agree that those two little 'uns need to be protected," he said. "Whoever it is that thinks they can come to my house – our house – and threaten, steal our livestock…whoever it is, they'll find out exactly who they're dealin' with." He straightened up to his full height, and she had a brief flash of a vision of him with his shirt sleeves rolled up, the wood-splitting axe hefted meaningfully in one hand. No, James Monroe was not the sort of man to be trifled with.

She felt flooded with such unexpected trust and confidence in him that it brought a blush to her cheeks and she averted her eyes.

He didn't seem to notice. Taking a seat on the rickety chair, which creaked alarmingly under his muscular weight, he paged through the letters again and gave a snort.

"Some of 'em aren't as crooked as others," he said. "I recognize a few of these names. My brother must have gone to everyone he could think of for money."

"How on earth did he end up so badly in debt?"

"He borrowed years ago to get this place – his wife wanted it. He would have done anything for her." His eyes flickered toward her, as though to weigh her reaction to the mention of the children's mother, but she kept her face calm and placid and he went on. "Roy was never much of a businessman. Couldn't make a living off the ranch, never kept track of his cattle. He always had bigger ideas than he had any right to. Dreamed of tearin' down this poor little cabin to build something bigger, for his wife, for the family they intended to have. He sent me drawings now and then of his newest schemes. He was sure, more's the pity, that the claim out back behind the house would give him all the riches he needed and then some." His mouth twisted. "And it gave him nothing – except an early grave."

She thought of the dark hole that was the mine and shivered.

"Well, then?" she asked quietly. "What do we do?"

James Monroe shook his head and folded the letters together in an unkempt wad.

"We wait," he said. "I haven't the means to repay any loans, never mind the inclination. But I'll be damned if I let some crook try and take this property, while I've breath in my body." His eyes fixed on her once more, weighing her up, gauging her reaction. "You're welcome to leave."

She took a deep breath.

"We agreed to a month," she said. "I'm not the type of woman to go back on my word – especially for the sake of the children. Yes, Mr. Monroe, we wait – and I daresay a month is long enough for things to end, one way or another."

He let out what might have been a laugh.

"Yes," he said. "One way or another."

CHAPTER 7

On the nineteenth of March, in the middle of Emma's promised month at the ranch, Emily suddenly became ill.

One moment, it was little more than a sniffle brought on, Emma supposed, by too long playing outside in what was still startling cold weather, since it was nominally springtime. But from the afternoon's sniffles came a rather wracking cough, and in the middle of the night Emma was startled awake by the noise of the little girl crying out, wordlessly.

She leapt from her bed and hurried down the hall to the room that Emily and Tom shared. There was a candle lit within; the light glimmered off Tom's gray eyes, turning them gold, as he stared wide-eyed at his sister's little cot. Emma's heart jumped to see the dark shape leaning over the little girl, and she clapped a hand over her mouth to stop her startled outcry, recognizing a split second later that it was James Monroe.

He was on his knees beside the girl and glanced over his shoulder at Emma.

"Stir up the fire in the kitchen, would you," he said. He stood up, lifting his niece with him, holding her tiny form in his arms easily. He stopped to give Tom a nod and smile. "Go on back to bed, Tom. She'll be all right, she just needs a little medicine."

Emma scurried downstairs to do as she was asked. Despite Monroe's reassurance to the little boy, she had a sinking feeling that the danger was far more real than expected. Monroe wasn't far behind her. She dragged forward the rocking chair, close to the hearth, expecting him to sink into it with his burden; instead, he nodded her toward it, and when she took a seat, settled Emily in her arms.

"She needs to be soothed a little," he said, his voice low. "She has a fever."

Indeed, the little girl's forehead was burning up. Emma closed her eyes tightly, wrapping her arms around Emily's limp frame, gently pushing the rocking chair into movement with her toes. It struck her then, with the suddenness of a bullet, how attached she had grown to these children; the thought of either of them becoming ill her heart stop. And should something worse occur…

No, she couldn't even think of it.

Monroe returned after a few moments. He moved with a quiet surety, setting a kettle to boil over the stirred fire, measuring out a generous spoonful of whiskey and slipping it between Emily's lips. He went to his knees in front of the chair; at the sudden, unexpected movement, Emma felt her heart jump. But he was only wringing out a cloth in the bucket of cold water he'd brought from the pump outside. He handed it to her, gesturing for her to place it on the girl's forehead, then bent again to another cloth, with which he bathed her hands and bare feet.

"We'll cool her down," he said, his tone slow and measured. "Little at a time, not too much of a shock."

"Will cold water do the trick?" She glanced involuntarily at the kettle, which was already beginning to steam.

He grinned suddenly.

"Cold for her," he said. "Hot for you and me. We'll be up for most of the night, I reckon. I'll make us some coffee."

It was now that she remembered Mrs. Henry's story – James Monroe had been a doctor, before he came here to take over his brother's ranch and look after his brother's children. She couldn't help but wonder how he had given up such a life so easily; after all, many years of schooling and hard work must have gone into his practice. But if he blamed that very practice, and himself, for the death of his wife and unborn child, perhaps the answer was in the question.

Perhaps he had already given up that life, long ago.

To see him bent on his task of caring for his niece, with a deftness and care in his touch that she never would have expected, was to see a completely different side of James Monroe. She spoke before she knew the words were coming.

"Mr. Monroe…"

He glanced up at her swiftly, then away. He did not speak. She hesitated, then took her courage in both hands and went on.

"I realized, just now, how very much these two children mean to me. How much I have come to care for them. Please – please tell me that she is going to be all right."

To her relief, he responded with a faint chuckle.

"Little 'uns catch chills and fevers all the time," he said. "Emily and Tom might seem frail, but they're stronger than you might think. They get that from their father's side." He sighed. "Tough as nails, all of us Monroes."

"Hmm," she said, not quite sure how to take this – and rather suspicious that he was somehow mocking himself, as well as his dead brother. In a sudden rush to change the subject to something less fraught with tension, she found herself instead treading on even more unsteady ground. "I suppose they don't much take after their mother, then – what happened to her, Mr. Monroe?"

Another swift glance, an unreadable expression in his eyes.

"You told me," he said after a moment, "that you know what it's like to lose both a mother and a father."

"Um – yes."

"You're an orphan, then? Like Emily and Tom?"

It was, she suspected, as much of an answer as to the fate of the children's mother as she was ever likely to get.

Her heart shied away from the thought of telling him her story – and yet, with such a pointed question, she could give him no less than the truth.

"No," she admitted. "Not completely an orphan."

He sat back on his heels for a moment, one eyebrow raising questioningly.

"Didn't take you for a fibber, Miss Potter."

"And indeed, I am not," she said, trying to quash her indignation so she didn't wake Emily. "I am without parent in this world, it's true, but there are other ways of losing your family than to the cold clutches of the grave."

He snorted. "They teach you poetry in Boston, I guess."

"As a matter of fact, they do – at the finishing school that I attended for three years. I was desperately unhappy there. I hated it. I wanted to go home to my family. I missed them so, and every night I would imagine what the day would be like when I finished my education and returned to the modest little house I'd been born in." The words drifted from her, dreamily, as though she had no control; the story wanted to be told.

"My years at school ended abruptly. One day, shortly after I turned fifteen, the headmistress told me that I had been expelled. It wasn't until later that I found out it was due to lack of payment. My parents owed the school for three months of education, as well as room and board; it baffled me as to why, for though we had never been affluent we had certainly never been penniless, either. When I arrived home later that day, I found out the reason."

She swallowed; her throat felt hot and dry. "My father had died the month before. My mother had had a breakdown and was unable to care for any of their responsibilities. But it was worse than that, you see – he had been ill for several months, though they had not told me, and in his illness had racked up quite a debt. A debt that we could not repay. On top of the debt owed to the school, we lost everything to the creditors – and still we owed.

"My mother was never of very strong character; I loved her, but I knew she was rather frail, even when I was just small. She did not speak to anyone for weeks, and when she did, she told me that I was to blame for my father's death, and the debt, too, for he loved me more than anything, and it was his insistence that I finish school that had led to his illness. She fled Boston and went to live with her sister, to be cared for to the end of her days – after telling me that she never wanted to see me again."

James Monroe let out a long slow breath, but did not look up at her.

She went on, determined now to get it all out.

"I stayed in Boston. Took on what work I could, determined to pay off the last of my father's debt – hoping that my mother might forgive me, when I did. It took me ten years. I worked day and night. But at last, the last of the debts were released, and I was a free woman for the first time in my adult life. I took the train to my aunt's house, explained to her what I had done. My mother refused to see me." She renewed her clasp on little Emily, finding as much comfort in the girl as she hoped Emily found in her arms. "I went back to Boston and applied to become a mail order bride. I was matched with your brother, Mr. Monroe, the very next day."

When she dared to look up, she found that he was watching her. But it was different, somehow; it didn't make her feel flushed, or as though she were doing something wrong, or as though she were desperate to escape from him. Instead, she felt as though she might cry. There was something new in his eyes, something she had not seen before – kindness.

"I reckon," he said, "as you're as near to family as you could get, you ought to call me James."

Tremulously, she smiled.

"Emma," she said.

He held out a hand, and she took it. His grasp was firm and warm and calloused, and she wondered whether his embrace would feel as all-encompassing, as though she had no choice but to surrender.

"Emma," he said, "I reckon I'd better make that coffee, now. After a tale like that, you're probably parched as a desert."

She was grateful to him – for the offer, of course, but even more so for the fact that he stood up and moved, away, letting her have a little space to herself to breathe. When his back was turned to her, she said, "I've never told the whole story to anyone."

She caught sight of his profile, the features dark and noble.

The corner of his mouth lifted in a wry half smile.

"I reckon," he said quietly, "that we've all got stories like that."

CHAPTER 8

The fourth week of Emma's residency had just begun when the knock at the door came.

They had just settled down to supper in the kitchen. No one was expected; no one ever came. Apart from her weekly visit to town for church, Emma had settled into a life that was as solitary as James Monroe preferred it to be. Now, though, they stared at each other over the table, wide-eyed.

"Who…" she started.

He stood up, his face grim.

"Stay here."

She waited until he had gone around the corner into the hallway, heading for the front door. Her heart hammering, suspicions whirling, she stood and crept to the kitchen door, pulling it open just a little to keep it from its habitual creak. The children watched her in silence. She held a finger to her lips, a warning that they did not need, and gestured for them to stay. Moving as silently as possible on her stockinged feet, she stepped down the hallway and craned her ear to listen.

The murmurs of voices were low. The voice of James – and others she did not recognize.

Suddenly his voice boomed out.

"My brother Roy is dead," he said. "As I understand it, far as the Lord is concerned, his debts are all paid."

"Be that as it may," said another voice, sharply, "but the Lord's a good bit more understanding than our boss is. Roy Monroe owes him a debt, and we're here to see it paid. We warned you."

James's voice was as cold as stone.

"Get off my property," he said.

"Ah, but it ain't yours, is it? It ain't Roy's, either – matter of fact, according to the contract he signed, it's ours – and you're trespassing."

Emma whirled and ran back into the kitchen, leaving behind the sound of the beginnings of a battle. Though her whole being longed to rush out to stand at James's side, to defend the house that had become her home, she knew that she had more use elsewhere – there were more important things to care for. She scooped Tom up hurriedly from his chair, carrying him to the door, slipping him through and gesturing Emily after him. The two children stood outside in the gathering dusk of the spring evening, turning peaky, wide-eyed looks on her.

She lowered her voice to a whisper.

"To the Browns," she said. "They're the closest neighbors – you know the way, Emily, don't you?"

The little girl nodded, her face pale. Of course, she knew the way, Emma thought, heartsick; she had gone there first, over a month before, after discovering the death of her father. No one had been home, then, and she had had to walk five miles into town. Emma could only pray that someone would be at home at the Browns' farm today.

"Go and tell them to ride for the sheriff's deputy," she said. "Or anyone they can send. Go now, children – quickly and quietly."

Bless them for their obedience, she thought, as they spun and ran off without further question. She blinked back tears; the last sight of them was of Emily reaching for her brother's hand, tugging him to keep up with her longer strides.

Then she closed the door as quietly as she could, and raced back toward the hallway, her heart in her mouth.

"James?"

"Oh, ho," crowed a voice in triumph.

She rounded the corner toward the front door; the sight that met her eyes was precisely what she had feared, and what she had expected. There were three men there to force the repayment of the loan; crooks, every one of them, she was certain of it. James could not hope to stand against them, despite his strength. Even now he was struggling with two of them, but at the sound of her voice he turned to face her, eyes wide with desperation.

"Emma!"

One of the other men landed a blow on his chin, and he slumped to the ground, eyes rolling back into his head. Emma felt a dart of fear in her chest – not for herself, though the man who seemed to be the leader turned toward her with a look in his eyes she did not like, but for James.

"Don't hurt him."

"We won't, little lady," the leader of the men chuckled, but she heard the lie as clear as day. "Provided he gives us what we want. He seems awful reluctant to do so – but I reckon you might help us persuade him."

He reached out and snatched her by the arm; taken by surprise, she almost fell into him as he tugged her viciously toward him. Recovering herself just enough, she regained her footing after her stumble, reared back on one foot, and brought the other down solidly on his.

"Damnation," he roared.

She lifted her free hand to slap at him, but found it trapped by his. He pushed her against the wall, pressing close.

"Let her go."

James had come to his senses; still sprawled on the floor, he pushed the second man out of the way and got to his feet, his eyes alight with fury. It was only the sound of a gun cocking that made him stop before he caught hold of Emma's assailant by the throat with both hands.

He froze.

The third man, who had scarcely moved during the entire episode, held a gun trained at him. Emma half expected to see an evil smile on his lips, the stuff of novels; but there was nothing there but a faint hint of exasperation.

"You're makin' this much harder than it has to be, Monroe," he said. "Your brother told our boss time and time again that he had a mine which was making him a fortune. Told him the money would be there any day, soon as he turned the gold in. Well, we're done with waitin'. We'll take the gold."

James's face was white.

"There is no gold," he said. "The mine's a bust."

The third man pursed his lips.

"That's too bad," he said. "We've got to have something to take back to our boss, you see, to amend the debt." He sighed regretfully. "I guess we'll just have to take the missus here instead."

Emma's captor laughed with all the evil delight that she would have expected from a classic fairy tale villain; despite herself, she cried out, and her voice was echoed by that of James.

"All right," he said, hands out, beseeching. "It's true. Roy did find gold, and he's been stockpiling it in the woods to avoid having to pay his debts. He spent the last six months lyin' about the claim, saying it was a bust. But he wrote me before he died and told me where it was. Let her go – let her go, and I'll show you where Roy hid it."

Even had Emma not known that this was a patent lie, she would have suspected as much. James Monroe was many things, but a convincing liar he was not; it showed in his paleness, in the slight trembling of his fingers. But greed was a powerful force, and after a moment of deliberation, it seemed to outweigh doubt.

The leader of the three cast one more contemptuous glance at Emma, then pushed her aside.

"All right," he said. "But she stays here. Freddy can watch her. She's collateral against your word, Monroe…" He grinned. "Too bad she wasn't collateral against your brother's loan, or maybe we'd all be home happy this very moment." From his holster, he pulled another pistol and jerked his chin at James. "Go on, Monroe. Lead the way."

James cast a last, desperate glance at Emma. She could not move her eyes from him; her heart was in her throat, trapping the words she longed to say. He was going away from her – and in her heart she was certain that she would never see him again. When the men discovered that he had lied, they would shoot him down like a dog, there in the woods.

But he was trapped like her. She only hoped that he understood that she had managed to help the children escape; she had seen those small dark figures running past, headed for the pathway leading to the road, while the villains had been so thoroughly engaged with the fight.

She closed her eyes and turned away.

The second man, who hadn't spoken, gestured her back toward the kitchen with his own pistol. She did as she was bid, realizing as she entered that the presence of four place settings would certainly alert him that there had been others present. Hastily, clattering the dishes together in her nervousness, she snatched the four plates and piled them haphazardly in the half-empty pot of soup, tossing spoons on top.

"Sit down."

"I was only clearing up a little..."

"Sit. Down."

She sat down, pulse jumping in her throat. He sat down, too, an expression of boredom on his face, and she wondered if he really had not noticed.

"Guess we've got a while to wait," he said sourly.

She nodded. "I suppose…you do this sort of thing often enough that…"

"No talking."

Emma pressed her lips together. The thing to do now, she knew, was to obey orders and not provoke him. If he hadn't realized that the children had been here and escaped, there was always a chance…

She thought of James, and her heart wrenched within her.

Just a chance.

The next half hour was the most tortuous time Emma Potter had ever experienced. Sitting in complete silence apart from the ticking of the clock, she fixed her eyes on the window and watched as the sunset ended and twilight set in, as thickly as fog. Her heart ached for the children – and for their uncle. They had already lost so much. Could the good Lord possibly allow them to lose what little they had left?

A far-off crack, like the sound of a branch breaking. She glanced up swiftly, and the villain stood, hefting his pistol in his hand. He frowned, his mind seeming to move slowly through the possibilities.

"I reckon…" he said, and that was all he had time for.

The first bullet whined through the window with a crash; Emma hit the floor and scrambled under the table without hesitation, without even a scream. The man with the gun shouted a curse which ended in a shout of pain; the kitchen door was flung open with enough force to rebound off the far wall, and suddenly her sanctuary was filled with rushing bodies. Among them, from her position crouched on the floor, she spotted two sets of very small bare feet.

"Emily! Tom!"

Somehow, she was out from her shelter, both children in her arms, pressing them close. She was crying, in great heaving sobs, but when she drew back enough to look at them, she was shocked to see that they were both beaming as though they had gone on the most exciting adventure of their lives.

Which was, she realized, true in a way.

She clasped them to her once more, and among the milling figures that filled the kitchen she spotted a familiar face.

"Jeremiah!"

The young shop boy gave her a firm nod and a bright smile.

"Good thinking, Miss Potter, sendin' those two little 'uns after the deputy. 'Course, he's not here at the moment, but

Mr. Brown rounded up the rest of us and here we are, ready to fight whoever needs fightin'." He gave a rather contemptuous glance to the man sprawled on the floor, whimpering as he clutched at the bullet wound in his shoulder. "Not that he needed much," he added darkly. He moved to the injured man and bound his legs and tied his hands with the rope hanging from his belt. The man screamed in pain.

"Jeremiah, there are two more men – and they have James!"

Through the hubbub that ensued in the wake of her gasping revelation, she managed to tell the tale. Before she knew it, she was being swept up with the children and deposited on the sofa in the sitting room, told to rest. The sofa was never used, and as she squirmed uncomfortably on the firm cushion, she suddenly understood why.

"But I can't simply stay here," she cried, leaping from the seat. "I must go with you." She took hold of Jeremiah's arm and pulled it down until she could reach it, stripping the pistol from his grip. "I can fight as well as anyone," she told him.

Jeremiah eyed her doubtfully.

"The little 'uns…" he started.

Emma turned to Emily and Tom, who sat close together on the sofa. Emily's arm was firmly around her little brother, and she gave a deep nod to Emma's questioning glance.

"We're safe here," she said. "Mrs. Brown will be here any moment."

Emma, overcome with pride and love, leaned down and kissed each of them on the forehead. Then she turned a look of triumph on Jeremiah, who gave a heartfelt sigh.

"Well, all right," he said. "I guess you've come this far, Miss Potter, it wouldn't be like you to turn back now."

As the posse made their way into the woods, the refrain echoed through Emma's mind again and again. I've come this far – I've come this far – and I won't turn back now.

I came here because of my engagement to Royal Monroe – I came here fleeing the sadness of my past.

I found more sadness here. But that wasn't all.

If I stay – if I stay – it will be because of Emily and Tom and James, because I love them all.

I'm going to stay.

I will have to convince James of it, I know – but I'm going to stay.

As soon as I find him.

Though some light still lingered in the skies, night fell as soon as they entered the thick forest. A few members of the posse bore lanterns, and the sight of the lights bobbing back and forth, disappearing suddenly behind the trunks of trees, made her feel almost seasick. She left Jeremiah behind, rubbing a thumb over the cold metal of the gun in her hand, and pressed out into the darkness on her own. All she wanted was to find the man she loved –

A sudden shout, and she turned toward it, breaking into a run. Pelting through the trees, she knew that she was in imminent danger – not just from the criminals who were demanding payment, but from the trees themselves. If she fell, she might twist her ankle…or break her neck. But there was light there suddenly, just ahead of her, and she redoubled her efforts, panting and winded but continuing onwards.

She burst into the clearing with a wild cry, and the three men, fighting closely in the dim light of the overturned lantern, turned to face her. She squeezed her eyes shut, lifted the gun, and pulled the trigger.

One shot.

Two.

Three.

It was over in a trice. She found out later that Jeremiah had followed her more closely than she had thought; he was scarcely a few steps behind her when the light appeared and had run almost at her side. The rest of the posse were not far away. The first shot had been hers, of course; the second had been Jeremiah's, aimed at the man in the lead; the third had caught his colleague in the leg.

Emma opened her eyes to find a familiar face just in front of hers – all the more familiar because of the black scowl that marked those familiar faces.

"James," she managed weakly.

His brow furrowed over the bridge of his noble nose.

"What the *hell* do you think you're doing, barging in here waving a pistol?"

He was bruised and bleeding. One dark eye was swelling up; she lifted a hand and touched it gently.

"That'll be a fine shiner in the morning," she said softly, scarcely aware of what she was doing.

James Monroe glared at her.

"The hell you say," he said, and pulled her into his arms. His kiss was just as she had imagined it, over and over, though she'd denied it to herself every time – fierce and passionate and true, and she was not sure what was more likely: if she might melt in his arms or burst into flames.

CHAPTER 9

The lawyer wore pince nez. Emma had not seen a pair of the strange little spectacles since her days in finishing school, where the dancing instructor sported a pair. They had kept falling off, as she remembered. She tried not to stare.

Mr. Donaldson removed the spectacles, tucked them in his pocket, and rubbed the bridge of his nose with his fingers.

"I'm afraid," he said, "that the letters are entirely legitimate."

Beside her, Emma felt James tighten up.

"All of them?"

"It appears so, yes. Some of them are more likely to be – ahem – criminally founded, as were the gentlemen so recently apprehended. I feel that you might safely discount those; when that underworld finds that the sheriff's eyes are closely on you, after the misadventures of their fellows, I doubt that you'll receive any more unwelcome visitors. It seems that your brother borrowed rather paltry amounts from a wide variety of sources, rather than large lump sums that might…well, land you in more hot water." He coughed genteelly. "But this one in particular, Mr. Monroe, is rather worrisome." He held up a letter, still folded. Emma did not recognize it, but it was evident from the way James drooped that he did.

"The bank," he said.

"The bank," Mr. Donaldson confirmed. "The ranch is entailed, I'm afraid. And the final date of repayment is upcoming rather sooner than any of us would like. In fact, if the loan is not repaid in full by the beginning of next month – April, that is – then ownership of the ranch defaults to the First National Bank. There is no appeal."

"But the children…"

Mr. Donaldson shook his head regretfully.

"Even," he said, "for the children."

He left soon after that, leaving Emma and James alone in the uncomfortable sitting room. Emma would rather have had the discussion in the comfort of the kitchen, suspecting that it would be unpleasant, but it seemed more proper to show the dignified lawyer into the sitting room instead. She remained where she was, on the hideous sofa, as James stood at the window, his hands clasped behind his back.

She cleared her throat.

"Well," she said. "What do we do?"

He shook his head.

"I have no control over what you do, Miss Potter," he said. "Heaven help the man who ever tries."

She couldn't help but be stung by his words; looking up, she was shocked to see that he had not even done her the courtesy of turning around to look at her.

"What on earth is that supposed to mean?"

"I always say exactly what I mean."

"But I don't understand it."

"I hardly think I'm to blame for your silliness."

His tone was calculated to offend. She leapt to her feet.

"How dare you, James Monroe. After everything we've been through…"

"You," he said, turning around at last, "have only been here the past four weeks. I reckon that must have been enough for you, don't you think? So, you head on back to Boston a free woman, as you've always longed to be, and leave me to take care of my kin."

She stared at him.

"You can't mean it."

"I told you, Miss Potter, I always say what I mean."

She hesitated. The coldness of his stare was convincing – but not quite convincing enough.

With her heart in her mouth, she stepped forward.

"You're trying to send me away because you think it will protect me."

He pressed his lips together and said nothing.

"In a few days, it will be April. The ranch will belong to the bank, and you will have nothing – you, and Tom, and Emily. You'll all be left with nothing. And you think that if you chase me away by being a beast, you'll save me from the same fate."

This landed home; she could see it by the way his eyes averted from hers. He was strong, no doubt, the biggest, strongest man she'd ever seen. But he had his weaknesses, too.

And she, she realized, was one of them.

"In a few days," he said heavily, "the month will be up. The month we agreed to, mind. You promised not to meddle."

"I never promised any such thing. I said I wouldn't be inclined to – but things have changed, James. Don't you understand? Things have changed, and a month doesn't matter a bit. A month is not enough." She reached out and took his hand. "Not for me."

He took in a deep breath and turned toward her.

A cry from the hallway stopped him just as he started to reach for her.

"It's Emily," cried Tom, pointing to the window, his face streaked with tears. "She's trapped!"

Tom in her arms, Emma raced for the mine in James's wake, her heart beating so swiftly that she worried it would take flight. It could not have been more than three minutes since any collapse in the mine; the cloud of dust was still settling. The mine had taken the life of Emily's father, she thought blankly. It could not take the life of Emily herself. She hugged Tom close to her.

"Where was she?" James asked the boy, voice terse with worry.

He pointed, then turned and buried his head in Emma's shoulder.

James glanced at Emma, swiftly, just enough to let her know that she was seen – and then he was gone, disappearing into the cloud of dust and the darkness of the cave.

She tried to shake the feeling that he had looked at her as though she were the last person he would ever see.

Tom weeping in her arms, she ventured closer to the mine, trying to soothe the little boy. How awful it must have been for him, to see his sister disappear into the depths of the darkness.

"Tom," she said, doing her best to keep her voice from quavering, "why did Emily go into the mine?"

It took a repeat of the question, soft but insistent, before she elicited any reply.

"She heard the man," the little boy managed through his tears, voice muffled against her shoulder. "We're gonna lose the ranch...Pa's ranch...she thought if she...found Pa's gold..."

Emma's heart clutched. The gold that Roy Monroe had spoken about so freely, the gold that his children must have heard him rhapsodize about, fantasize over, the gold that formed the foundation of his dreams – the gold that did not exist. Or if it existed it had never been found.

And Emily had gone in search of it – and the mine had collapsed on her.

She heard her name called from within the depths, and her heart quailed for a shameful moment before she responded. She set Tom down and got to her knees before him.

"You must stay here," she told him. "Stay and wait. If your uncle James and I don't return in…in ten minutes, or if you hear another loud noise or see a cloud of dust, then you must run for the Browns. Do you understand?"

Biting his lip, the little boy nodded. Emma pressed a kiss to his forehead and turned away.

She went into the mine.

It was shocking, how quickly the light grew small, as though the cave was eating it. But after scarcely thirty seconds of moving forward blindly, her reaching hands found the stalwart shape of James Monroe. He turned and took her hands in his, speaking quickly.

"She's on the other side of this fall. Unhurt, thank God. She told me so. I've moved enough that I think I can lift it. I'll hold it up, and you must reach under and pull her through. Do you understand, Emma?"

"Y-yes."

He pressed a kiss to her face, blindly in the dark, on her cheek.

"Be brave," he whispered. She tried to force her eyes to see through the dark; it was little more than shapes, but it was something. The moving bulk that must be James bent down, and with a grunt another shape joined his, blending into one. There was a deeper darkness below it, and she scrambled forward, on her hands and knees, and reached out until she grasped something warm and living.

She pulled.

Emily came sliding out from under the fall, and Emma scooped the girl up in her arms, heedless of the fact that the seven-year-old was nearly as tall as she was. She cried something wordless to let James know that they were free and ran for the light. It grew larger and larger and suddenly they were back out in the world, free and alive. Emily's eyes were so wide and blue, and her face so dark with dirt and dust, that Emma could have laughed.

Then there was a crashing sound behind them, and she froze, turning around.

It went on for far longer than it ought to have. Nothing should fall for such a length of time – nothing short of an entire mountain.

In the silence that followed it, she stood with Emily in her arms. She felt Tom's hand clutching at her skirts while they waited. For the first time since the moments before her mother's ultimate rejection, Emma closed her eyes tightly and prayed.

Please, Lord…please let him be safe…please let him come back to me…

From the depths of the cave there came a dusty chuckle.

The figure that came into the light was almost unrecognizable, so covered was it in grime. The exertion of moving rocks and rubble to get to his niece had slicked James with sweat, and dirt had stuck to it, seeming to cover every inch of him in something very much like mud. But his teeth gleamed white in the midst of it, and he laughed as he came back into the world.

She ran forward, heedless of any lasting danger, heedless of the dirt, and pulled him into her arms. He clung to her tightly, and she took his dirty face in her hands and kissed him.

James Monroe pulled back, grinning at her.

"A little forward, ain't you, Miss Potter?"

"James Monroe, if you don't…"

He kissed her again, then put her back a step and brought his hand up between them.

"Look," he said hoarsely. "Look."

She didn't know what she was looking at, at first. She wouldn't have picked it out of the dirt. But there was something to the rock he held in his hands; something unusual. A whitish streak cutting through, like marble, like fat on a roast.

"Roy was right," James said. "Guess we owe him an apology."

The realization struck home, and she clasped him anew.

"Enough?" she asked in a whisper, as though it were something holy. "Is there enough to save the ranch?"

"Enough to save the ranch, pay off anyone else, and keep us goin' for a while, I reckon. Took that last fall to bring it crashing down practically on my head." He chuckled, and the sound ran straight through her to her toes. "Guess I'm a miner, now."

"Oh, James! That's it – just enough is all we need, isn't it? To stay together, to be safe and happy. To be a family…"

She felt the children press close, arms wrapped around their knees; felt Emily's slight shuddering and knew that it was from disbelief.

"Are you sure?" James asked her, holding them all close. "Are you sure you won't change your mind and go back to Boston? It's not too late."

She wrapped her arms a bit more firmly around him and smiled.

"The hell you say."

CHAPTER 10

The promised month was well up, and Emma Potter was packing her things.

How strange, she thought, feeling rather distant – how strange to be gathering up everything she had ever owned, so soon after she had done just that, back in Boston. How strange to think of how things had changed, between now and then. Once upon a time – it couldn't possibly be a matter of only months, could it? Once upon a time, she had decided to strike out and start her life anew. She had accepted an engagement to a stranger and traveled more than a thousand miles to keep her word.

Then she had discovered that he was dead, and that he had been a liar, and….well, everything else that had happened. It was exhausting just thinking about it.

She closed her trunk, stood away from it for a moment, and looked out the window vaguely. She had grown quite attached to this place, she knew; the numbness that she felt in her heart was only a means of protection. She didn't want to cry, not anymore.

The time for tears had passed along with the collapse of the cave.

There were better things ahead, she told herself – and the fact that she did not yet know what they were needn't be any deterrent. She picked up her valise, took a deep breath, and left the little bedroom to go down the stairs.

No one was waiting for her. The cabin was empty. She took stock of everything as she left; the sparse rooms so much tidier than when she had first arrived. Everything had become so familiar, so dear. Now, she would leave it all behind.

She did not take a last look into the kitchen, the place that had become a haven. Instead, she turned toward the front door. Another deep breath, and a step toward the future – and whatever waited for her there.

What waited – or rather who – was her husband.

He gave her a grin. She was still growing accustomed to seeing such a look on his face, so similar to his photograph. It made him look much younger. Happier, too.

He held a hand out to her, and she took it gladly.

"Ready, Mrs. Monroe?"

She sighed and smiled.

"As ready as I will ever be, I suppose."

It wasn't far to go. The new house had been built, with startling swiftness over the past month, not far from the old one. Together, James and Emma walked toward it. Inside, their children waited.

Halfway there, she turned and looked back over her shoulder. The old place would stay where it was. A memento of the memories. A place for the children to remember their father. A sight that would remind Emma of all her blessings.

One day, it would succumb to the creeping hand of time and fall to pieces; and James Monroe would come along and split the pieces, a little bit at a time, to bits of wood small enough to fit inside their stove. The memories of the past would keep them warm on long winter nights, while their little family sat together and talked and laughed and told each other stories - the stories that needed to be told.

The End

CONTINUE READING...

Thank you for reading **Colorado Mountain Bride!** Are you wondering **what to read next?** Why not read *The Banker's Pianist Bride?* **Here's a peek for you:**

The last few notes died away in the breathless hush that filled the room, and Cora Reed bowed her head over her hands in her lap. For a long moment, she sat in utter stillness, hardly even breathing, while she waited for what always came at the finale of her performances.

Sometimes, it started as a ripple. Other times, a smattering. Tonight, at this poignant appearance, it erupted all at once, as though the hearts and minds of the hundred men and women in the audience were moved to show their appreciation in unison. The applause was not there one moment and simply appeared the next, seemingly designed to raise Cora and her fellow musicians to their feet.

The violinist took his bow; the man at the bull fiddle did as well. Cora alone sat with her head down, refusing to look up and see the evidence of the adoring audience.

Perhaps if she had done this more often, she thought resentfully, she would not be in this predicament. Mr. Connor – well, evidently, he preferred it when females knew their place.

In her heart, though, she knew that there was no true way that she could have avoided this situation – no true way that she could have managed to keep this from being her last performance at the West Street Music Hall. Her fate had been signed and underscored from the first moment that Mr. Connor stopped by to investigate the possibility of purchasing the business from the previous owner, the kindly if rather doddering Mr. Richards. Mr. Richards had hired Cora when she was sixteen, after a deft display of her talent at the ivories and had never given her a moment's trouble about anything.

She had known from the first sight of Mr. Connor that he was a different breed entirely; decades younger than Mr. Richards, he was yet somehow far more old-fashioned, and the idea of a lady performing her talents onstage, especially alongside gentlemen musicians, was outrageous to his sensibilities. No, Mr. Connor had decided at once that she must go; she had seen it in his eyes, in the small distasteful pinch of his mouth, and her heart had sunk to her boots.

Visit HERE To Read More!

https://ticahousepublishing.com/mail-order-brides.html

THANKS FOR READING!

If you **love Mail Order Bride Romance,** **Visit Here**

https://wesrom.subscribemenow.com/

to find out about all **New Susannah Calloway Romance Releases! We will let you know as soon as they become available!**

If you enjoyed *Colorado Mountain Bride*, would you kindly take a couple minutes to leave a positive review on Amazon? It only takes a moment, and positive reviews truly make a difference. Thank you so much! I appreciate it!

Turn the page to discover more Mail Order Bride Romances just for you!

MORE MAIL ORDER BRIDE ROMANCES FOR YOU!

We love clean, sweet, adventurous Mail Order Bride Romances and have a lovely library of Susannah Calloway titles just for you!

***Box Sets — A Wonderful Bargain for You!*ced*

https://ticahousepublishing.com/bargains-mob-box-sets.html

Or enjoy Susannah's single titles. You're sure to find many favorites! (Remember all of them can be downloaded FREE with Kindle Unlimited!)

Sweet Mail Order Bride Romances!

https://ticahousepublishing.com/mail-order-brides.html

ABOUT THE AUTHOR

Susannah has always been intrigued with the Western movement - prairie days, mail-order brides, the gold rush, frontier life! As a writer, she's excited to combine her love of story with her love of all that is Western. Presently, Susannah lives in Wyoming with her hubby and their three amazing children.

www.ticahousepublishing.com
contact@ticahousepublishing.com

Made in United States
Troutdale, OR
10/30/2025

40908226R00062